My
Pocket
Guide

MICHIGAN

By Carole Marsh

Correlates with Michigan Social Studies Content Standards
SSCS

THE **MICHIGAN** ExperiencE

The GALL🌐PADE GANG

Carole Marsh	Doug Boston	Pam Dufresne
Bob Longmeyer	Jill Sanders	Cranston Davenport
Chad Beard	William Nesbitt, Jr.	Lisa Stanley
Cecil Anderson	Kathy Zimmer	Antoinette Miller
Steven Saint-Laurent	Wanda Coats	Victoria DeJoy
Karin Petersen	Terry Briggs	Tena Simpson
Billie Walburn	Jackie Clayton	

Published by GALLOPADE INTERNATIONAL

www.michiganexperience.com
800-536-2GET • www.gallopade.com

Gallopade is proud to be a member of these educational organizations and associations:

NSSEA

ASD

SHOPA MEMBER
School, Home, & Office Products Association

Other Michigan Experience Products

• The Michigan Experience!
• The BIG Michigan Reproducible Activity Book
• The Michigan Coloring Book
• My First Book About Michigan!
• Michigan "Jography": A Fun Run Through Our State
• Michigan Jeopardy!: Answers and Questions About Our State
• The Michigan Experience! Sticker Pack
• The Michigan Experience! Poster/Map
• Discover Michigan CD-ROM
• Michigan "Geo" Bingo Game
• Michigan "Histo" Bingo Game

A Word From the Author... (okay, a few words)...

Hi!

Here's your own handy pocket guide about the great state of Michigan! It really will fit in a pocket—I tested it. And it really will be useful when you want to know a fact you forgot, to bone up for a test, or when your teacher says, "I wonder . . ." and you have the answer—instantly! Wow, I'm impressed!

Get smart, have fun!
Carole Marsh

Michigan Basics explores your state's symbols and their special meanings!

Michigan Geography digs up the what's where in your state!

Michigan History is like traveling through time to some of your state's great moments!

Michigan People introduces you to famous personalities and your next-door neighbors!

Michigan Places shows you where you might enjoy your next family vacation!

Michigan Nature - no preservatives here, just what Mother Nature gave to Michigan!

All the real fun stuff that we just HAD to save for its own section!

Michigan Basics

Michigan Geography

Michigan History

Michigan People

Michigan Places

Michigan Nature

Michigan Miscellany

Who Named You?

Michigan's official state name is...

State
Name

Michigan

Word Definition

OFFICIAL: appointed, authorized, or approved by a government or organization

Statehood: January 26, 1837

Michigan was the 26th state to join the United States.

Michigan will be on a state-commemorative quarter in the year 2004. Look for it in cash registers everywhere!

Coccinella noemnotata is my name (that's Latin for Ladybug)! What's YOURS?

What's in a Name?

Michigan got its name from the Ojibwa Indians. This tribe is also known as the Chippewa. They called Michigan, *michigama*, which means "great waters." This could be because four of the five Great Lakes touch Michigan's borders. Those four Great Lakes are Lake Superior, Lake Huron, Lake Erie, and of course, Lake Michigan.

State Name Origin

Michigan is the only state that is divided into two distinct parts. The northern part is known as the Upper Peninsula, and the southern part is the Lower Peninsula.

5

Who are you calling Names?

State Nicknames

Michigan is not the only name by which our state is recognized. Like many other states, Michigan has some nicknames, official or unofficial!

The Great Lakes State

Wolverine State

Water Wonderland

While Michigan is known as the Wolverine State, there's no evidence that any of these animals lived here in the wild. Most likely, just their hides became known in the state when French fur traders brought them in to trade with the Indians.

Lakes are great!

State Capital:
Lansing

Since 1847

In 1805, Detroit was named the Territory of Michigan's first capital, but the state constitution said that the legislature could name a new permanent capital in 1847. After a lot of arguing, they chose Lansing because of its central location. At that time, Lansing only had a sawmill and a few cabins. New factories and businesses came to the new capital.

When Lansing was named the state capital, its name was almost changed to Michigan. That would have made it Michigan, Michigan!

Word Definition

CAPITAL: a town or city that is the official seat of government
CAPITOL: the building in which the government officials meet

State Government

Who's in Charge Here?

Michigan's GOVERNMENT has three branches:

LEGISLATIVE   **EXECUTIVE**   **JUDICIAL**

State Government

The legislative branch is called the General Assembly.

Two Houses:
THE SENATE (38 members elected for four-year terms); HOUSE OF REPRESENTATIVES (110 members elected for two-year terms)

A governor, lieutenant governor, secretary of state, and 16 cabinet heads

SUPREME COURT (seven members) Appellate Court, followed by Circuit Courts and Courts of Claims. Also District Courts and Probate Courts

In the mid-1990s, the executive branch's department went through some major changes. The Department of Environmental Quality was added, and the Department of Community Health was formed from the former public health, mental health, and Medicaid programs.

When you are 18 and register according to Michigan laws, you can vote! Please do so! Your vote counts!

State Flag

Salute the flag!

Michigan's current state flag was adopted in 1911. It features a bald eagle above the coat of arms. An elk is on the left side of the state seal, and a moose is on the right. The first state flag featured a portrait of the first governor, Stevens T. Mason.

As you travel throughout Michigan, count the times you see the Michigan flag! Look for it on government vehicles, too!

State Seal & Motto

State Seal

The state seal of Michigan was adopted in 1835. It is featured on the state flag. The bald eagle on top of the coat of arms shows that Michiganders recognize that the national government is the chief authoritative body.

State Seal & Motto

Word Definition

MOTTO: a sentence, phrase, or word expressing the spirit or purpose of an organization or group

State Motto

If you seek a pleasant peninsula, look about you.

Michigan's state seal also features the Latin word Tuebor, which means "I will defend." Above the eagle is the U.S. motto *E Pluribus Unum*, (Out of many, one.)

Michigan's state motto is translated from Latin...

Si quaeris peninsulam amoenam, circumspice.

" Michigan is actually two pleasant peninsulas."

Birds of Red Feathers

The robin was adopted as the state bird in 1931.

State Bird

Robins are members of the thrush family. European colonists gave the red-breasted bird its name after a smaller and brighter-chested bird they knew from their homelands.

Robins are found in every state except Hawaii.

Robins grow to be about 9 inches (22 cm) long. They eat berries and insects.

WHITE PINE

"Woodman, spare that tree!"—George Pope Morris

When Michigan was first settled, the white pine was important to the budding lumber industry. However, very few white pine forests exist today. As the trees were cut down and new trees were replanted, they had a hard time surviving diseases, such as white pine blister rust. The white pine was adopted as Michigan's state tree in 1955.

APPLE BLOSSOM

"...And apple-blossoms fill the air." —Alan Seeger

The Michigan legislature realized how important agriculture is in the state and has established many trade organizations. Apple growers get their support from the Michigan Apple Committee.

In 1897, the apple blossom became the official state flower of Michigan. Apples are an important crop to the state economy. Other fruits grown in the state are cherries, pears, blueberries, grapes, peaches, and plums.

Wild Wolverines

Wolverine

Michigan's nickname is the Wolverine State, but you are not likely to ever see a wolverine anywhere in Michigan...except at the zoo! Wolverines are not native to the state, but live in Canada and northern Minnesota. Someone just got the idea that they may have lived in Michigan, too. Early fur trappers probably traded wolverine pelts with Michigan Indians.

Wolverines are not known for being lovable. In fact, they have been known to chase bears and cougars from their food! Wolverines also protect themselves by spraying out a strong odor, like a skunk's. So, maybe it's good that they're not the official state animal!

Michigan could have been nicknamed the Beaver State. During the state's territorial days, beavers were very common, but over-hunting almost wiped them out of Michigan.

I sure wouldn't want to tangle with a wolverine!

Painted Turtle

Michigan schoolchildren asked their legislators to name the painted turtle as the state reptile. In 1995 they were successful and it was adopted.

State Reptile

Painted turtles get their name because their heads, tails, shells, and limbs feature brightly colored patterns, making them look like someone took a brush and red or yellow paint and decorated them!

Male turtles have longer, thicker tails than females do. They also have longer claws.

Male painted turtles get the attention of females by fluttering their long claws in front of the females' faces!

RIDDLE:

What did one painted turtle say to the other?

ANSWER:
I can't recognize your shell—is it a Picasso or a Van Gogh?

15

Petoskey Stone

State
Stone

Coral generally grows in warm waters, and during prehistoric times, Michigan was warm enough for coral to grow there. Parts of Michigan were covered by an ancient sea. The coral reef that existed in the northern part of the Lower Peninsula has turned to stone that is called Petoskey stone.

In 1965, this rock-hard coral was adopted as the state stone of Michigan!

Coral is a small marine animal with a bony skeleton. When it dies, the skeleton remains, and after thousands of years they pile up and make a reef!

"Those skeletons are millions of years old."

Isle Royale Greenstone

The state gem's real name is *Chlorastolite*. It is sometimes called Isle Royale Greenstone. In 1972 it was named the state gem. These gems really are green! Greenstone is most often found in the Upper Peninsula.

State Gem

Greenstone

"The Isle Royale Greenstone is fit for a king—or even a princess!"

Greenstone is a metamorphic rock, which means it is formed from other rocks after they go through major changes. Changes in temperature and pressure cause the changes.

17

Kalkaska Sand

The state soil can be found in 29 of Michigan's counties, and it covers nearly 1 million acres (400,000 hectares)! While Michigan has almost 500 different types of soil, Kalkaska soil is the most common. It was named the official state soil in 1990.

There is also a county in Michigan named Kalkaska. It was the site of a large lumber village, Deward. After 11 years the lumber mill closed and the village became a ghost town.

"Let's build a castle out of Kalkaska sand!"

Burly Bears

Black Bear

A Bear All Its Own

Michigan has its own bear—the Michigan Black Bear. Unlike some varieties of animals, the number of Michigan Black Bears may actually be increasing. One reason may be because these bears stay out of sight! Sometimes people can live in bear country for years without ever seeing one!

Twenty areas have been set aside since 1972 for wilderness areas. The black bear and other animals can live safely there.

Brook Trout

–Salvelinus fontinalis–

State Fish

Brook trout are excellent game fish, and with all the water in Michigan, there are plenty of opportunities to reel them in!

At first, brook trout were mainly found in the Upper Peninsula waters, but in the 1900s, they spread to the Lower Peninsula.

The trout was named Michigan's official state fish in 1965, but in 1988 it was made more specific when the brook trout was adopted.

Michigan Trout

Put a trout fillet on foil.
Drizzle with lemon juice.
Sprinkle with salt and pepper.
Add shredded smoked ham
and broil fish until done.

State Map

The State of
Michigan

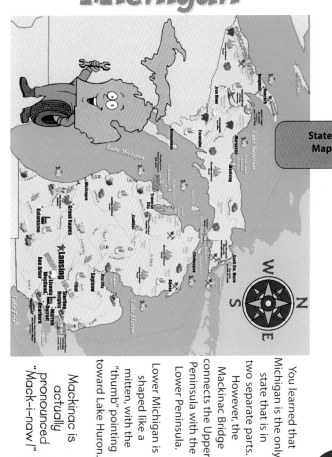

You learned that Michigan is the only state that is in two separate parts.

However, the Mackinac Bridge connects the Upper Peninsula with the Lower Peninsula.

Lower Michigan is shaped like a mitten, with the "thumb" pointing toward Lake Huron.

Mackinac is actually pronounced "Mack-i-naw!"

State Location

Michigan is one of the Great Lakes states. Except for the southern borders of both the Upper and Lower Peninsulas, the other borders are formed by Great Lakes.

State Location

THE CONTIGUOUS UNITED STATES

Michigan

Word Definition

LATITUDE: Imaginary lines which run horizontally east and west around the globe
LONGITUDE: Imaginary lines which run vertically north and south around the globe

On The Border!

These border Michigan:

States: Wisconsin   Ohio   Indiana

Country: Canada

Bodies of water: Lake Superior, Lake Michigan, Lake Erie, and Lake Huron

I'll Take the Low Road...

**East–West
North–South
Area**

The Lower Peninsula stretches 286 miles (460 kilometers) from north to south, and 200 miles (322 kilometers) from east to west.

**Total Area: Approx. 96,705 square miles
Land Area: Approx. 56,809 square miles**

The Upper Peninsula stretches 334 miles (538 kilometers) from east to west and 215 miles (346 kilometers) from north to south.

This is a compass rose. It helps you find the right direction on a map!

N

W E

S

You Take the High Road!

HIGHEST POINT
Mount Arvon—1,979 feet (603 meters)

Some sources list another mountain, Mount Curwood, as the highest point in the state, but it only rises 1,978 feet (602.8 meters).

LOWEST POINT
At Lake Erie—572 feet (174 meters)

25

State Counties

I'm County-ing on You!

Michigan is divided into 83 counties.

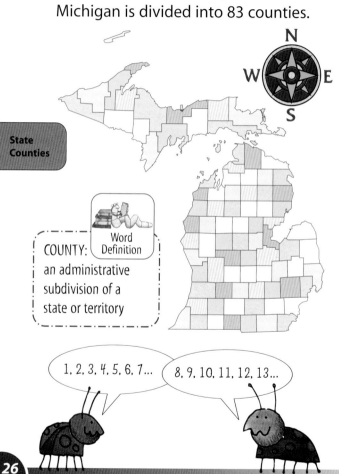

COUNTY: an administrative subdivision of a state or territory

Word Definition

1, 2, 3, 4, 5, 6, 7...

8, 9, 10, 11, 12, 13...

Natural Resources

It's All Natural!

Forests make up about 18,253,000 acres (7 million hectares) in Michigan. More than 90 percent of the Upper Peninsula is covered by timber.

Word Definition

NATURAL RESOURCES: things that exist in or are formed by nature

Natural Resources

Minerals and rocks:

Copper

Iron Ore

Natural Gas

Petroleum

Limestone

Salt

Sand

Gravel

Water

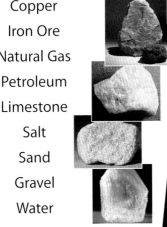

Because Michigan is surrounded by more Great Lakes than any other state, fresh water is always nearby. Some experts claim that Michigan is the most fortunate place on earth because of its ready access to water.

Weather, Or Not?!

Michigan's moist, temperate climate makes it a great place for growing crops. Temperatures range from 10° to 25°F (-12° to -4°C) in the Upper Peninsula in the winter and 58° to 75°F (14° to 24°C) in the summer. In the Lower Peninsula, it's warmer: 19° to 32°F (-7° to 0°C) in winter, and 63° to 84°F (17° to 29°C) in summer.

Weather

Highest temperature: 112°F (44°C), Mio, July 13, 1939

°F=Degrees Fahrenheit °C=Degrees Celsius

Lowest temperature: -51°F (-46°C), Vanderbilt, February 9, 1939

During the spring, the snow melts and rivers overflow and Michigan becomes a muddy mess. Years ago, when Michigan had a lot of dirt roads, schools would close for a week during the spring so the buses wouldn't get stuck in the mud. The kids called this Mud Week!

Topography

BACK ON TOP

Michigan's topography has something for everyone. There are flatlands, hills, mountains, beaches, islands, forests, and even swamps!

Michigan has been described as having a "wrinkled" appearance. This was caused by the glaciers that came through more than 10,000 years ago. These wrinkles are actually rippling hills.

Word Definition

TOPOGRAPHY: the detailed mapping of the features of a small area or district

Sea Level

100 m | 328 ft

200 m | 656 ft

500 m | 1,640 ft

1,000 m | 3,281 ft

2,000 m | 6,562 ft

5,000 m | 16,404 ft

The northwest corner of the Upper Peninsula is the only place in the state where you can find mountains.

King of the Hill

Michigan's highest point, Mount Arvon, is part of the Gogebic Range, which runs along the western edge of the state's border with Lake Superior.

Western Michigan is also the location of some impressive sand dunes. As the glaciers moved southward over the area, they crushed soft rocks in their path and left behind lots of sand. Winds blowing from Lake Superior piled the sand in dunes. As the sand blew about, it cut off bays from Lake Michigan and created many inland lakes.

The Sleeping Bear Dunes are on Lake Michigan. The highest one is 465 feet (142 meters).

"Ain't no mountain high enough..."

Major Rivers

A River Runs Through It!

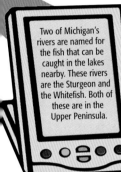

Two of Michigan's rivers are named for the fish that can be caught in the lakes nearby. These rivers are the Sturgeon and the Whitefish. Both of these are in the Upper Peninsula.

Major Rivers

Here are some of Michigan's major rivers.

Upper Peninsula
- Escanaba
- Manistique
- Menominee
- Ontonagan
- Tahquamenon

Lower Peninsula
- Au Sable
- Grand
- Detroit
- Muskegon
- Kalamazoo
- Raisin
- Saginaw

Gone Fishin'

Major Lakes

Major lakes in Michigan include:

UPPER PENINSULA
- GOGEBIC
- INDIAN
- MANISTIQUE

LOWER PENINSULA
- HOUGHTON LAKE
- BLACK LAKE
- BURT LAKE
- CHARLEVOIX LAKE
- CRYSTAL LAKE
- HIGGINS LAKE
- MULLET LAKE
- TORCH LAKE

In Michigan, you are never more than 6 miles (10 kilometers) from a river, stream, or lake.

Waterfalls are common in the Upper Peninsula. There you can see more than 150, but in Lower Michigan, there is only one—the Ocqueoc, near Rogers City.

Word Definition

RESERVOIR: a body of water stored for public use

ARE YOU A CITY MOUSE... OR COUNTRY MOUSE?

Have you heard these wonderful Michigan city, town, and crossroad names? Perhaps you can start your own collection!

Cities & Towns

LARGER TOWNS:
- Detroit
- Grand Rapids
- Warren
- Flint
- Lansing
- Sterling Heights
- Ann Arbor
- Livonia
- Dearborn
- Westland
- Kalamazoo

SMALLER TOWNS:
- Cadillac
- Coldwater
- Flushing
- Zilwaukee
- Inkster
- Parchment
- Paw Paw
- Pontiac
- Rome
- Holly

"I wouldn't drive my Cadillac into Coldwater."

One Michigan town is called Zilwaukee. Its founders hoped people would get confused and move there instead of Milwaukee, Wisconsin. People didn't buy it, though. Zilwaukee only has about 2,000 residents!

Transportation

Major Interstate Highways

Interstates 75, 69, 196, and 94. About 120,000 miles (193,000 kilometers) of roads connect Michigan with the rest of the country.

Railroads

Railroads are not used as often today as they were a century ago. The trucking and airline industries are used more often, but Michigan does have about 10 cities with passenger train services.

Major Airports

Michigan has international airports in Detroit, Flint, Grand Rapids, Saginaw, Kalamazoo, and Lansing.

Canals

Hundreds of iron-ore carriers transport their load on the canal at Sault Sainte Marie, or the Soo Locks. It is one of the world's busiest waterways. Other chief ports are in Detroit, Escanaba, Muskegon, Port Huron, Marine City, and on the Saginaw River.

3000 BC	Mound builders arrive in Michigan
1618	Frenchman Étienne Brulé is first European to visit Michigan
1634	Jean Nicolet arrives in Michigan
1668	Jacques Marquette sets up European settlement
1680	Fur trade flourishes in Upper Great Lakes
1763	French and Indian War ends
1787	Michigan becomes a part of the Northwest Territory
1813	Indians lose their claim to large amounts of land
1835	Michigan adds Upper Peninsula after squabble with Ohio
1837	Michigan becomes 26th state in the Union
1840s	Logging and copper and iron mining begin
1854	Republican party gets its start in Michigan
1855	The Soo Ship Canal and Locks are finished
1860s	Civil War–Michigan remains loyal to Union
1896	First Oldsmobile and Ford cars are built in Detroit
1963	Fourth and present state constitution is ratified
1974	Michigan resident Gerald Ford becomes 38th president
1988	Auto industry has its third-best sales year ever
1992	Congress protects Michigan's rivers with Michigan Scenic Rivers Act

Timeline

On to the 21st Century!

Mackinac Island was the base for John Jacob Astor's American Fur Company.

35

Here come the humans!

Thousands of years ago, ancient peoples inhabited Michigan. They may have originally come across a frozen bridge of land between Asia and Alaska. If so, they slowly traveled east until some settled in what would one day become the state of Michigan. Around 3000 BC they learned to make ax heads and spear points from copper.

These early people were nomadic hunters who traveled in small bands. They camped when seasons offered hunting, fishing, and fruit and nut gathering.

Native Americans Once Ruled!

Early Michigan Indians built large earthen structures we call mounds. Some of these structures still stand today west of Grand Rapids. These structures date back 2000 years. The mounds may have been built for ceremonial or religious purposes.

Early Indians

Word Definition

WAMPUM: beads, pierced and strung, used by Indians as money, or for ornaments or ceremonies.

Land Ho!

The first Europeans to reach Michigan traveled through the Great Lakes by canoe. These explorers were searching for a "Northwest Passage" through North America to the Pacific Ocean. Although they never found a sea route to the Pacific, they did claim the newly discovered land for France. Voyageurs (French trappers and traders) traveled all over Michigan's many waterways. By the 1700s, many of the lakes and rivers had been mapped by the French.

Exploration

Explorers, missionaries, and adventurers came from Europe on ships in the 1500s.

Ahoy, Mate!

Settlement

Home, Sweet, Home

Roman Catholic priests established the first missions in Michigan. These missions were built to convert the Indians to Christianity. The first mission was built in 1660 by Father René Ménard at Keweenaw Bay in the Upper Peninsula. Many early missionaries knew how to make maps. Their notes were used to help chart the Great Lakes.

Jacques Marquette, a Jesuit priest, built a church called Sault Sainte Marie that became Michigan's first permanent European settlement.

Settlement

Antoine de la Mothe Cadillac is known as the founder of Detroit. He commanded a group of Frenchmen and built Fort Pontchartrain on the present-day site of Michigan's largest city.

In 1825, the Erie Canal opened in New York. This made travel much easier and brought many more people to Michigan.

Some of the names of Michigan cities were taken from these early explorers. Marquette and Cadillac are two.

Furs, Farms, and Forests!

The first commercial enterprise in Michigan was fur trading. Indians and early explorers hunted and trapped animals for their skins, or pelts. The furs were then traded or sold and made into clothing and hats. Fur trading was big-time business for about 200 years.

In the mid-1800s, loggers came to harvest Michigan's bountiful woodlands. For almost 70 years, they stripped large amounts of trees. Forests have been replenished and now cover more than half of Michigan.

Furs, Farms, and Forests!

Michigan's main crops include cherries, navy beans, cucumbers, blueberries, apples, plums, carrots, celery, mushrooms, tomatoes, grapes, pears, strawberries, sweet corn, onions, potatoes, livestock, and dairy products.

Copper and iron mining were also important. The mining boom started in the mid-1800s in the Upper Peninsula.

MILK

YOGURT

Paul Bunyan

Paul Bunyan is a Michigan legend. The legend says that Paul was a lumberjack, and he was very big. He also had a large friend named Babe. Babe was a giant blue ox who was twice as big as all outdoors. Paul dug out the Great Lakes so that Babe would have a place to drink.

Paul Bunyan

Some say the legends of Paul Bunyan are based on a real-life timberman—Fabian Fournier of Saginaw, also known as Saginaw Joe. He was known for his great strength and wood cutting ability.

Do you know why hotel owners made lumbermen wear slippers when they stayed overnight? To protect the carpets from their heavy hobnail boots!

Freedom!

Some settlers in the New World felt that England ignored their ideas and concerns. In 1775, the colonies went to war with England. On July 4th, 1776, the Declaration of Independence was signed.

Revolution

In 1783, the Revolutionary War finally ended. The new United States wasn't quite strong enough to make the British leave Michigan. They finally surrendered their forts to the Americans in 1796. The British retook two forts during the War of 1812, but only held them for a year. The American flag has proudly flown ever since that time!

There were no important Revolutionary War battles fought in Michigan. However, the British used their fort at Detroit to give supplies to the Indians who were helping them fight the Americans.

Slaves and Slavery

OF HUMAN BONDAGE

Michiganders were bitterly opposed to slavery. The easterners who had settled Michigan were against slavery, and the Europeans who later moved to Michigan also thought it was wrong. The issue of slavery and states' rights led to the Civil War. The Underground Railroad, which helped slaves escape to freedom, had several "stations" in Michigan.

Slaves and Slavery

The present-day Republican political party had its beginnings in Michigan and one of the reasons it was formed was to oppose slavery!

In 1865, the 13th amendment abolished slavery in the United States.

Word Definition

ABOLITIONIST: person who believed slavery was wrong and should be abolished.

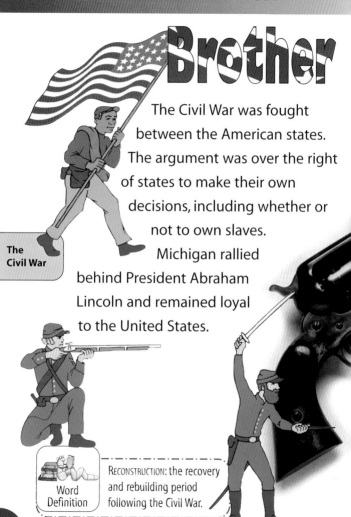

Brother

The Civil War was fought between the American states. The argument was over the right of states to make their own decisions, including whether or not to own slaves.

Michigan rallied behind President Abraham Lincoln and remained loyal to the United States.

The Civil War

RECONSTRUCTION: the recovery and rebuilding period following the Civil War.

Word Definition

The Civil War

As many as 90,000 Michiganders fought for the Union in the Civil War. More than 14,000 gave their lives fighting for the causes they believed in!

The Civil War

In 1863, the Emancipation Proclamation, issued by U.S. President Abraham Lincoln, freed the slaves still under Confederate control. Some slaves went to Northern states to work in factories.

Get It In Writing!

Declaration of
Independence, 1776

Northwest Ordinance,
1787

Famous
Documents

U.S. Constitution,
1789

First State Constitution,
1835

Present State
Constitution, 1963

WELCOME TO AMERICA!

Michiganders have come to Michigan from other states and many other countries on almost every continent! As time has gone by, Michigan's population has grown more diverse. This means that people of different races and from different cultures and ethnic backgrounds have moved to Michigan.

Immigrants

In the past, many immigrants have come to Michigan from France, England, Canada, Holland, Ireland, Poland, and Germany. More recently, people have migrated to Michigan from Asia and the Middle East. Only a certain number of immigrants are allowed to move to America each year. Many of these immigrants eventually become U.S. citizens.

Disasters & Catastrophes!

1881

A great fire roared through the Upper Peninsula. It was the first major disaster that the Red Cross handled. Ten years before, in 1871, the community of Holland was destroyed by fire.

1896

A tornado ripped through Oakland killing 47 people. In 1953, tornadoes again struck Michigan, killing 142 people. In 1980, tornadoes struck Kalamazoo, wiping out parts of the city.

Disasters & Catastrophes

1913

The Freshwater Fury, a violent storm, blew through Port Huron killing 270 people. Ten ships carrying ore sank.

Hold on!

A tornado is a high narrow column of air usually shaped like a funnel and spins very fast!

1932

One third of Detroit workers lost jobs during the Great Depression. A "hunger march" riot occurred at the Ford plant in Dearborn. Four people were killed.

1943

Racial violence in Detroit killed 34 people and left 700 injured, and erupted again in 1967 killing 43 people.

Legal Stuff

1835

Michigan and Ohio squabbled over ownership of the Toledo Strip. The U.S. Congress gave the strip to Ohio, and awarded Michigan the western Upper Peninsula.

1917

The 18th Amendment to the U.S. Constitution, or Prohibition, outlawed production and consumption of alcohol. Mobsters, like Detroit's Purple Gang, illegally imported alcohol from Canada to Detroit.

1929

Legislation was passed to allow cities to buy fireworks—but not individuals.

1932

Michigan governor, Wilbur Brucker, called for an eight-day bank holiday to prevent banks from going out of business during the Great Depression.

1963

Michigan's present state constitution was approved, including "home rule." This allowed self-government for local communities.

Women & Children

1919

Michigan ratified the 19th Amendment to the U.S. Constitution giving women the right to vote.

1920

The 19th Amendment to the U.S. Constitution became law.

Women & Children

1934

Helen Richey, the first woman pilot to carry airmail, lands in Detroit.

1942

The All American Girls Professional Baseball League was created. Flint's Sophie Kurys set five all-time league records in 1946. Penny Marshall made a movie, *A League of Their Own,* all about the girls and their bats, gloves, and baseballs!

Batter up!

Wars

Fight!, Fight!, Fight!

Wars that Michiganders participated in:

- French and Indian War
- Revolutionary War
- War of 1812
- Civil War
- Spanish-American War
- World War I
- World War II
- Korean War
- Vietnam War
- Persian Gulf War

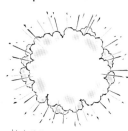

Wars

Marvelous Machines from the Motor City

It all started with a few pistons, cylinders, and camshafts. Ransom E. Olds and Henry Ford both built gasoline-powered automobiles in 1896. Around the turn of the century, Michigan's factories began producing cars. In 1913, Henry Ford sped things up by installing assembly lines to help build the Model T—his most popular car.

Awesome Autos

Detroit was the main hub for automobile production, but factories popped up in Flint, Pontiac, and Lansing. Car production went into high gear and helped Michigan grow and prosper!

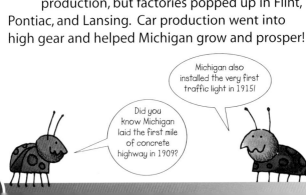

Michigan also installed the very first traffic light in 1915!

Did you know Michigan laid the first mile of concrete highway in 1909?

Indian Tribes

- Chippewa (Ojibwa)
- Menominee
- Wyandot
- Potawatomi
- Ottawa
- Miami

The Ottawa, Chippewa, and Potawatomi formed a group known as the Three Fires. Although their everyday lives were different, they all spoke Algonquian dialects and shared similar cultural traditions.

The Indians of Michigan could not have known that the coming of the white man would mean an end to the way of life they had known for hundreds of years!

Ottawa Chief Pontiac formed the Pontiac Alliance, the largest group, dedicated to defeating the white man in North America.

Here, There, Everywhere!

Frenchman ÉTIENNE BRULÉ explored the Great Lakes. He was the first European to see Michigan.

Frenchman JEAN NICOLET also sailed the Great Lakes. He was looking for a passageway to China.

In 1660, FATHER RENÉ MÉNARD built a mission at Keweenaw Bay in the Upper Peninsula.

Explorers and Settlers

FATHER JACQUES MARQUETTE built Sault Sainte Marie, the first permanent European settlement in Michigan.

RENÉ-ROBERT CAVELIER, Sieur de La Salle built forts along the shores of the Great Lakes.

Bon Voyage!

N
W — E
S

State Founders

Founding Fathers

These people played especially important roles in early Michigan!

In 1701, ANTOINE DE LA MOTHE CADILLAC, a soldier and fortune-seeker, established Fort Pontchartrain on the present-day site of Detroit. He is known as the founder of the city of Detroit.

LEWIS CASS, territorial governor, accompanied a large group to explore and map Michigan and present-day Wisconsin.

HENRY R. SCHOOLCRAFT was the geologist for the Cass expedition. He later settled in Sault Sainte Marie, married a part-Chippewa woman, and wrote about Indian life in the North Woods.

Founding Mothers

State Founders

MARIE-THERESE GUYON CADILLAC was the wife of Antoine de La Mothe Cadillac and the first European woman to come to Michigan.

ELIZABETH MARGARET CHANDLER was a Quaker who lived in Lenawee County. She promoted the abolitionist cause and established the Logan Female Anti-Slavery Society, the first women's anti-slavery society in Michigan.

NANCY HARKNESS LOVE founded the flight school at Vassar College and created the Women's Auxiliary Ferrying Squadron later called the Women's Air Force Service Pilots or WASPS.

Famous African-Americans

SOJOURNER TRUTH was born a slave named Isabella Baumfree. She escaped to freedom and fought for abolition, women's rights, and prison reform. She also traveled the U.S. as an evangelist.

COLEMAN YOUNG was elected mayor of Detroit in 1973. He was the city's first African-American mayor. He successfully persuaded leaders in the business community to invest in Detroit. In 1979, he received the Jefferson Award, and the National Association for the Advancement of Colored People awarded him the Spingarn Medal.

ROSA LEE PARKS is known as the "mother of the civil rights movement" for her courage in standing up for human rights. In 1955, she refused to give up her seat to a white man on a bus in Montgomery, Alabama. Her bravery sparked a bus boycott in Montgomery as well as protests all across America. In 1957, she moved to Detroit. In 1999, Rosa Parks was presented the congressional Gold Medal—the highest award a civilian can receive.

Famous African-Americans

MALCOM X was an African-American nationalist leader who was from Lansing. He was a powerful speaker and became a very influential civil rights leader.

R-E-S-P-E-C-T

During the 1950s, a very musical young African-American named Berry Gordy, Jr. worked for the Ford Motor Company. While he was off, he wrote songs and recorded some new singing groups. That's how Motown Records was born.

Motown Records had a very special sound—a blend of pop music and black gospel. Gordy had a gift for finding exciting new talent in the black communities of Detroit. Groups such as the Supremes, the Jackson Five, Smokey Robinson and the Miracles, the Temptations, Martha and the Vandellas, and Gladys Knight and the Pips recorded for Motown Records. Other artists, such as Mary Wells, Stevie Wonder, Marvin Gaye, and Tammi Terrell were a part of Motown, too!

The Music of Motor Town

Aretha Franklin was named one of Michigan's natural resources in 1985. With a beautiful voice that covers four octaves, it's no wonder. She was born in Tennessee, but grew up in Detroit. She was the daughter of a gospel preacher and was coached by many family friends, including Mahalia Jackson. Aretha's songs include "Respect," "Natural Woman," and "Chain of Fools." She has 21 gold records and 15 Grammy awards. The "Queen of Soul" was inducted into the Rock and Roll Hall of Fame in 1987.

Famous Michigan Sports Figures:

TY COBB–baseball hall of famer

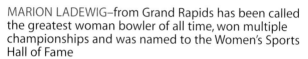

MEGAN FITZGERALD, KATHY KUBICKI, ANNE BOYD, and LAURA MURPHY–very fast women runners

BARRY SANDERS–running back with the National Football League Detroit Lions

MARION LADEWIG–from Grand Rapids has been called the greatest woman bowler of all time, won multiple championships and was named to the Women's Sports Hall of Fame

JOE DUMARS–guard for Detroit Pistons professional basketball team, known for his athletic skills and community service

GORDIE HOWE–hockey player for Detroit Red Wings Professional Hockey team

Sports Stuff

JOE LOUIS–professional boxing champion, held heavyweight title for 12 years

ISAIAH THOMAS–guard for Detroit Pistons professional basketball team, received multiple Most Valuable Players awards

HAVE YOU EVER SEEN A TRIPLE PLAY IN BASEBALL? Neal Ball, of Grand Haven, played second base for the Cleveland Indians and on July 19, 1909 caught a line drive (out #1) with runners on first and second. He stepped on second for a double play (out #2) and tagged the runner coming from first (out #3)! Wow! Can we see an instant replay?

Entertainers

- ★ PABLO CASALS–cellist

- ★ AARON COPLAND–composer

- ★ TOMMY JAMES AND
  THE SHONDELLS–musical group

- ★ LILY TOMLIN, GILDA RADNER–actresses, comediennes

- ★ TIM ALLEN–actor, comedian

- ★ BETTY HUTTON, LINDA HUNT, MEREDITH BAXTER,
  MARLO THOMAS, ELLEN BURSTYN, JULIE HARRIS,
  KIM HUNTER–actresses

- ★ SONNY BONO–Sonny and Cher musical duet

- ★ CASEY KASEM–radio personality, inducted into Radio
  Hall of Fame

- ★ DELLA REESE–singer and actress

- ★ THE WINANS–contemporary gospel
  singing family

- ★ GEORGE PEPPARD, JASON ROBARDS, ROBERT WAGNER,
  HARRY MORGAN, DANNY THOMAS, TOM SELLECK–actors

FRANCIS FORD COPPOLA–screenwriter
and director

ED MCMAHON–entertainer,
television host

Authors

- **RICHARD HAFT**–novelist
- **SARAH SMITH**–short story writer
- **WILL CARLETON**–poet, founded poetry magazine, *Every Where*
- **VERNA NORBERG AARDEMA VUGTEVEEN**–children's author, won Caldecott Medal for *Why Mosquitoes Buzz in People's Ears*
- **JOHN VOELKER**–writer, pen name was Robert Traver, best known for *Anatomy of a Murder*
- **TOM LYNCH**–poet
- **JUDITH ANN GUEST**–writer
- **BRUCE CATTON**–historian, writer, won Pulitzer Prize
- **JOYCE CAROL OATES**–writer, educator, used Michigan as the setting for many of her novels
- **CONSTANCE FENIMORE WOOLSEN**–writer
- **THEODORE ROETHKE**–poet, won Pulitzer Prize
- **RING LARDNER**–journalist and author
- **JAMES OLIVER CURWOOD**–novelist
- **EDGAR GUEST**–journalist, poet, popular radio host

Authors

Ernest Hemingway used the lake region of northern Michigan as the setting for some of his early short stories.

nom de plume: French for pen name, a fictitious name a writer chooses to write under instead of his/her real name

Artists

DIEGO RIVERA–painter, his industrial theme mural is displayed at the Detroit Institute of Arts

J.M. STANLEY–painter who not only used canvas, but also painted on buggies, carts, and farm wagons

GILDERSLEEVE HURD–artist, created country scenes on walls of houses

JAMES O. LEWIS–printer, engraver, explorer, helped design the state seal

LOWELL BOILEAU–artist, one of first in Michigan to have a website

GILDA SNOWDEN–painter

CARL MILLES–sculptor born in Sweden, taught at Cranbrook Academy of Art

Some people objected to the subject matter that Diego Rivera chose for his famous industrial mural. It seemed to say that technology was oppressing the workers. The arts community stood behind Rivera to make sure that his work was preserved!

Very Important People

BETTY FORD–First Lady

JOHN JACOB ASTOR–prominent fur trader, and real estate tycoon

LEE IACOCCA–automobile manufacturer

PONTIAC–Ottawa chief, brilliant military leader

GEORGE ARMSTRONG CUSTER–army general, killed at the Battle of Little Big Horn

FATHER GABRIEL RICHARD–Catholic priest who served in U.S. Congress, pastor of St. Anne's Church in Detroit

RANSOM ELI OLDS–created Michigan's first automaking company, the Olds Motor Works

FANNIE PECK–established the Housewives' League which dealt with problems facing African-American women

JOHN AND HORACE DODGE–built auto parts for Ford and Olds, later started their own car company

CHARLES HACKLEY–timber baron who donated money to his hometown of Muskegon to build a school, park, library and other public buildings

CHARLES WILLIAM POST–developed Postem, one of the first commercially prepared breakfast cereals

Very Important People

More VIPs

SAMUEL POKAGON–Potawatomi leader, poet, author of books and magazine articles that told about his Native American heritage

WILLIAM DURANT–industrialist, "Godfather of the Automobile Industry"

ALBERTUS VAN RAALTE–Dutch preacher, founded the community of Holland, Michigan

JOHN AND WILLIAM KELLOGG–physician and manufacturer of cereals respectively

HERBERT DOW–founder, Dow Chemical Company

CHARLES LINDBERGH–aviator, made first solo transatlantic flight

MINORU YAMASAKI–architect, designed many of Detroit's buildings

CAROLINE BARTLETT CRANE–first woman editor of a city newspaper in the nation, supported a bill to regulate meat and dairy processing plants which passed in 1903 by the Michigan legislature

S.S. KRESGE–merchant, founder of Kresge variety stores (now K-mart Corporation)

More VIPs

Good Guys/Bad Guys

GOOD GUYS/GALS

ANNA HOWARD SHAW was a minister, doctor, and suffragist. She worked with Susan B. Anthony for passage of the 19th Amendment giving women the right to vote.

JULIA WHEELOCK worked with the Michigan Relief Association during the Civil War. People called her "Michigan's Florence Nightingale" because of the long days she spent nursing the wounded and the sick.

RALPH BUNCHE was born in Detroit. He helped establish the United Nations. In 1950, he became the first African-American awarded the Nobel Peace Prize.

Good Guys/ Bad Guys

PEARL KENDRICK was a bacteriologist whose work produced the first successful vaccine to fight whooping cough.

BAD GUYS/GALS

The Unabomber, **TED KACZYNSKI**, studied at the University of Michigan before he left technology behind, moved to the woods, and built his murderous bombs. He was captured by the authorities after his brother turned him in.

In 1901, **LEON CZOLGOSZ**, of Seney, assassinated William McKinley, the 25th U.S. President, in New York.

Political Leaders

GERALD R. FORD–38th U.S. President

JAMES COUZENS–mayor of Detroit, U.S. senator

RUTH THOMPSON–first woman elected to the U.S. Congress from Michigan

STEVENS T. MASON–first governor of Michigan

THOMAS E. DEWEY–lawyer, politician, governor of New York

FRANK MURPHY–mayor of Detroit, governor of Michigan, U.S. Attorney General, Supreme Court justice

CHASE SALMON OSBORN–governor of Michigan, fought to protect the woodlands of Michigan

MARTHA WRIGHT GRIFFITHS–U.S. Congresswoman, first woman elected lieutenant governor in Michigan

Political Leaders

HAZEN S. PINGREE–mayor of Detroit, governor of Michigan

GEORGE ROMNEY–governor

ARTHUR HENDRICK VANDENBERG–U.S. senator

G. MENNEN WILLIAMS–governor, chief justice of the Supreme Court

CANDACE S. MILLER–first woman to be elected secretary of state in Michigan

Keeping the Faith

CHURCHES

Carlton Center Church, Hastings

Guardian Angels Church, Manistee

Our Savior's Evangelical Lutheran Church, Manistee

First Congregational Church, Manistee

Old Mission Church, Old Mission

Mission Church, Fort Mackinac

Old Mariner's Church, Detroit

Saint Mary Catholic Church, Monroe

Word of Faith International Christian Center, Southfield

Bethel African Methodist Episcopal Church, Detroit–
this church was formed in 1839 and housed the first public
school for African-American children

SCHOOLS

Michigan State University, East
Lansing–first agricultural school in the nation

University of Michigan, Ann Arbor–was
the first state university to admit women

Churches and Schools

The world's largest crucifix is located in the town of Indian River. It is 55 ft (17 m) high and 22 ft (7 m) wide!

Wayne State University, Detroit

University of Detroit, Mercy

Western Michigan University,
Kalamazoo

Eastern Michigan University,
Ypsilanti

Central Michigan University,
Mount Pleasant

Northern Michigan University,
Marquette–training site for 23
Olympic sports events

Historic Sites and Parks

A FEW OF MICHIGAN'S HISTORIC SITES INCLUDE:

★ **HERITAGE HILL HISTORIC DISTRICT,** Grand Rapids

★ **NORTON INDIAN MOUNDS, GRAND RAPIDS**–group of 12 mounds located on the east bank of the Grand River

★ **CHARLTON PARK VILLAGE,** Hastings

★ **WHITE PINE VILLAGE,** Ludington

★ **GRAND HOTEL,** Mackinac Island–this enormous white structure opened in 1887 and is still in operation

★ **IRON MOUNTAIN IRON MINE,** Vulcan

A FEW OF MICHIGAN'S PARKS INCLUDE:

★ **MACKINAC ISLAND**–a historic state park since 1895; popular tourist site since before the Civil War

★ **FAYETTE,** near Escanaba–a ghost town-turned-state park

★ **WARREN WOODS NATURAL AREA,** Three Oaks

★ **MACKINAC MARITIME PARK,** Mackinaw City

★ **MILL CREEK STATE HISTORIC PARK,** Mackinaw City

★ **CHIPPEWA NATURE CENTER,** Midland

Historic Sites and Parks

Home, Sweet Home!

Early Residency

★ **GOVERNOR'S MANSION**, Marshall–built before the capital was moved from Detroit to Lansing

★ **PENDLETON-ALEXANDER HOUSE**, Marshall–built in 1835; known for its decorative trim

★ **HONOLULU HOUSE**, Marshall–exotic residence built in 1860 for Abner Pratt, U.S. consul to Hawaii

★ **MEYER-MAY HOUSE**, Heritage Hill–a Frank Lloyd Wright Prairie-style structure built in 1908

★ **STUART HOUSE**, Mackinac Island–1817 residency now displays various historical artifacts

★ **JOHN BURT HOUSE**, Marquette–an 1858 simple structure built of sandstone

★ **BENJAMIN BRADLEY HOUSE**, Midland–a Gothic Revival structure built in 1874

Home, Sweet Home!

★ **CHARLES W. NASH HOUSE**, Flint–built in 1890, this was the home of the founder of Nash Motor Company

★ **MOROSS HOUSE**, Detroit–built in the 1840s; oldest brick dwelling in the city

★ **FISHER MANSION**, Belle Isle–built in 1927; rambling Spanish eclectic structure

★ **MEADOW BROOK HALL**, Fair Lane–built in 1929; lavish 100-room English Tudor style mansion

Forts and Battles

Some of Michigan's Forts

- **Fort Gratiot**, Port Huron–built during the War of 1812
- **Fort Saint Joseph**, Port Huron–built by fur trader Daniel Greysolon, sieur Duluth
- **Fort de Buade**, Saint Ignace–built by French in 1680s
- **Fort Holmes**, Mackinac Island–built by the British in 1814 on the highest point of the island
- **Fort Mackinac**, Mackinac Island–built of stone by the British in 1781
- **Fort Michilimackinac**, Mackinaw City–built by the French

Some of Michigan's Battles

Forts and Battles

- **Battle of Bloody Run**, near Detroit–1763 skirmish between Pontiac and his Indian forces and the British at Fort Detroit
- **Battle of Raisin River**, Monroe–bloodiest battle ever fought on Michigan soil; 1813
- **Battle of Lake Erie**–1813; American naval forces defeated the British fleet, regaining control of the water routes to the East

Libraries

Check-out the following special state libraries! (Do you have a library card? Have you worn it out yet?!)

- **Detroit Public Library**–adorned with beautiful murals and housed in a Renaissance Revival Building; one of the largest and most progressive in the U.S.
- **Monroe County Library**–contains an extensive collection of Custer memorabilia
- **University of Michigan Library**, Ann Arbor–one of the largest in the nation
- **Library of Michigan**, Lansing–state library
- **The Gerald R. Ford Library**, Grand Rapids–holds the papers of the former president

Libraries

Debra Bonde of Livonia wanted to provide reasonably priced books for blind children. She founded Seedlings, a non-profit organization, in 1984. They provide books for 40,000 blind children nationwide.

Zoos & Attractions

- **Coppertown U.S.A.**, Calumet–recreated miner's village
- **Whitcomb Conservatory**, Belle Isle Belle Isle Aquarium
- **Delaware Mine**, Fort Wilkins State Park–former copper-mining operation
- **Michigan Space Center**, Jackson
- **Binder Park Zoo**, Battle Creek
- **Abrams Planetarium**, Lansing–housed at Michigan State University
- **Potter Park Zoo**, Lansing
- **Detroit Zoo**
- **Hidden Lake Gardens**, Tipton–arboretum

Zoos & Attractions

LION

Museums

- **The Ann Arbor Hands-On Museum**
- **Michigan Historical Museum**, Lansing
- **Fort Saint Joseph Museum**, Niles
- **Netherlands Museum**, Holland
- **Michigan Maritime Museum**, South Haven
- **Public Museum of Grand Rapids**
- **Fire Barn Museum**, Muskegon
- **Marine and Harbor Museum**, Beaver Island

- **Fort de Buade Museum**, Saint Ignace
- **Michigan Iron Industry Museum**, Marquette
- **Man, Time, and Environment Museum**, Midland
- **Dossin Great Lakes Museum**, Belle Isle
- **Tuskegee Airmen Museum**, Fort Wayne
- **Henry Ford Museum**, Dearborn

Lest We Forget

A few of Michigan's monuments and memorials:

- **ADAM CROSSWHITE MONUMENT**, Marshall–marks the site of the cabin of a fugitive slave from Kentucky

- **BEAUMONT MEMORIAL**, Mackinac Island–honors Dr. William Beaumont, the Army surgeon who made important observations of the human digestive system during the 1820s

- **BAGLEY MEMORIAL FOUNTAIN**, Detroit–a granite pavilion with carved lion's-head fountains; designed by Henry Hobson Richardson

- **CUSTER STATUE**, Monroe–erected in 1910 to commemorate his role in the Gettysburg campaign

Monuments
& Memorials

One day I'll have a monument named after me!

That will be one small monument!

73

The Arts

The Show Must Go On!

★ **Interlochen Arts Academy**, Traverse City–full-time boarding school for the arts; boasts 23 Presidential Scholars–more than at any other high school in the nation

★ **Temple Theatre**, Temple–built in 1926, it seated 2,196 and boasted plush surroundings; in 1977 it closed, only to be reopened in 1980, dressed in its original opulence

★ **Music House**, Acme–housed in an old granary, this music house contains a collection of music boxes, organs, and nickelodeons as well as one of the largest pipe organs ever built

The Arts

To be... or not to be involved in the arts — that is the question. What is your answer?

PROPS

Michigan touches more Great Lakes than any other state: Lake Michigan, Lake Huron, Lake Erie, and Lake Superior. There are two national lakeshores in Michigan. Pictured Rocks National Lakeshore is located on Lake Superior while Sleeping Bear Dunes National Park is located on Lake Michigan.

Michigan has more lighthouses than any other state. Here are a few:

Grand Traverse Lighthouse, Leland

Old Mackinac Point Lighthouse, Mackinac Island

Rock Harbor Lighthouse, Isle Royale

Copper Harbor Lighthouse, Copper Harbor

Old Presque Isle Lighthouse, north of Alpena

Lakeshores & Lighthouses

Roads, Bridges & Ports!

Roads...

Whitefish Bay Scenic Byway–traces the shoreline of Lake Superior's Whitefish Bay

Cherry Orchards Drive–from Cross Village to Traverse City

Pierce Stocking Scenic Drive–winds atop sand dunes with views of Lake Michigan

Bridges...

The **Mackinac Bridge** is the third longest suspension bridge in the nation. It links the two peninsulas of Michigan. It is often called the "Mighty Mac."

The **Sault Saint Marie Bridge** is one of three bridges that link Michigan with Canada.

Midland Foot Bridge was built in 1981 and is located in Chippewassee Park. This bridge spans two rivers and connects three different shorelines!

Roads
Bridges
& Ports

Ports...

Detroit   Muskegon
Escanaba   Bay City
Marquette

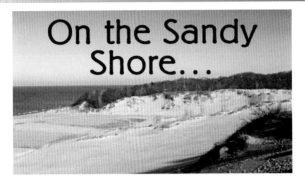

On the Sandy Shore...

The sand dune system of Lake Michigan starts in Indiana and extends almost all the way to the Straits of Mackinac, covering 275,000 acres (111,375 ha). It is the largest system of freshwater dunes in the world. In 1989, the legislature passed a law to protect 70,000 acres (28,350 ha) of the most fragile dunes that were in danger of being destroyed, due to misuse.

The **Sleeping Bear Dunes** rise close to 500 feet (151m) above Lake Michigan. The dunes are named after a Chippewa legend of a sleeping bear. The mama bear swam to the Lake Michigan shoreline and fell asleep waiting for her two cubs swimming behind her. The two cubs are now called North Manitou Island and South Manitou Island.

Sand Dunes of Michigan

Do I hear snoring?!

ANIMALS OF MICHIGAN

Michigan's animals include:

Beaver
Elk
Bobcat
Deer
Black Bear
Gray Wolf
Mink

Moose
Opossum
Otter
Porcupine
Rabbit
Raccoon
Skunk
Squirrel
Weasel

Michigan is home to 500 moose that weigh more than 1,000 pounds (450 kg) each! Wow!

Take A Walk On the Wild Side

Some endangered animals of Michigan are:

Gray Wolf
Kirtland Warbler
Cougar
Indiana Bat
Peregrine Falcon
Barn Owl

Keeping track of Kirtland Warblers is easy! The male birds never stop singing!

Wooow! This is so exciting!

Wildlife Watch

Birds

YOU MAY SPY THESE BIRDS IN MICHIGAN!

Bald Eagle
Barn Swallow
Blue Jay
Crow
Finch
Grouse
Hawk
Hummingbird
Partridge
Pheasant
Quail
Robin
Wild Turkey

A hummingbird's wings beat 75 times a second—so fast that you only see a blur! They make short, squeaky sounds, but do not sing.

Insects

Don't let these Michigan bugs bug you!

Ant
Butterfly
Cicada
Cricket
Dragonfly
Grasshopper
Honeybee
Katydid
Ladybug
Mayfly
Praying Mantis
Stick Insect
Whirligig Beetle
Yellowjacket

Bumblebee

Ants

Butterfly

Praying Mantis

Ladybug

Grasshopper

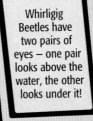
Whirligig Beetles have two pairs of eyes – one pair looks above the water, the other looks under it!

Insects

Do we know any of these bugs?

Maybe... Hey, that ladybug is cute!

Fish

Whitefish
Salmon
Lake Trout
Chub
Yellow Perch
Catfish
Carp
Sturgeon
Muskie

Fish

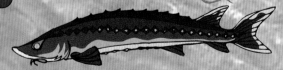

Pond Critters

Bullfrogs
Crayfish
Eels
Leeches
Muskrats
Pond Snails
Salamanders
Toads
Turtles
Water Shrews
Water Snakes

Doctors once tried to cure sick patients by "bleeding" them with leeches!

Pond Critters

83

Building Blocks

Minerals are the building blocks of all rocks.
A mineral can be large, but most are tiny.

Some minerals you may find in Michigan:

- **Iron pyrite**
- **Quartz**
- **Calcite**
- **Kaolinite**

Some rocks you may find in Michigan:

- **Petoskey stone**–state stone
formed from an ancient coral reef
- **Sandstone**
- **Mudstone**
- **Conglomerate**
- **Shale**
- **Quartzite**
- **Meteorites**
- **Peat**

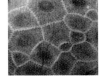

Rocks and
Minerals

Rock and Roll!

TREEMENDOUS!

THESE TREES GRACE THE STATE OF MICHIGAN:

Maple
Pine
Spruce
Hemlock
Red cedar
Willow
Elm
Beech
Cherry
Birch
Aspen
Sassafras
Oak
Hawthorn

Trees

Flowers

Are you crazy about these Michigan wildflowers?

- Violet
- Trillium
- Wild Geranium
- Columbine
- Lady's Slipper
- Black-eyed Susan
- Indian Paintbrush
- Buttercup
- Goldenrod

Flowers

"Flower power!"

Cream of the Crops

Michigan's principal agricultural products:

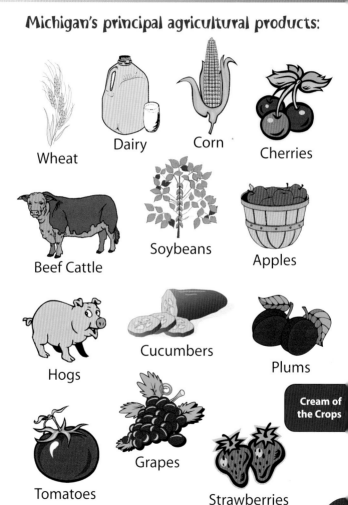

Wheat

Dairy

Corn

Cherries

Beef Cattle

Soybeans

Apples

Hogs

Cucumbers

Plums

Tomatoes

Grapes

Strawberries

Cream of the Crops

First/Big/Small/Etc.

1869

Detroit was the first city to assign individual telephone numbers.

1893

Marie Owen became the first woman appointed as a police officer.

1913

Detroit's Henry Ford instituted the first assembly line.

1945

Grand Rapids became the first city to add fluoride to its drinking water.

The Grand Hotel has the longest porch in the world, measuring **800 feet** (243 meters)!

Festivals

Snowmobile Festival, Boyne City and Copper Harbor–held in mid-March

Maple Syrup Festival, Shepherd and Vermontville–held in April

Highland Festival, Alma–Memorial Day weekend

Grand Prix, Detroit–held in June

National Cherry Festival, Traverse City–held in early July

State Fair, Detroit–held in late August

Mackinac Bridge Walk, from St. Ignace to Mackinaw City–held on Labor Day

Red Flannel Festival, Cedar Springs–held in October

Festivals

Holidays

Calendar

Martin Luther King, Jr. Day, *3rd Monday in January*	Presidents' Day, *3rd Monday in February*	Memorial Day, *last Monday in May*
Independence Day, *July 4*	Columbus Day, *2nd Monday in October*	Veterans Day, *November 11*
Michigan celebrates its admission to the U.S. on January 26th.	Thanksgiving, *4th Thursday in November*	Christmas, *December 25*

What's your favorite holiday?

Bug Day!

Famous Food

You can find the following foods in Michigan...

Yumm, yumm. This is great!

- Perch
- Rhubarb pie
- Cereal
- Pasty

- Whitefish
- Gerber baby food
- Little Caesar's Pizza
- Domino's Pizza

- Cherry Pie
- Coney Dog
- Chocolate fudge

Lets dig in!

MICHIGAN WORKS!

Michigan has a diverse economy with three major industries: manufacturing, farming, and tourism.

Detroit is famous for its automobile manufacturing. Ford Motor Company is one of the main auto manufacturers.

Michigan's Great Lakes are a major part of their trade. The state has many ports and is often called "America's fourth seacoast." Most of the shipments in and out of Michigan's ports are bulk commodities such as iron, coal, and limestone.

The opening of the Saint Lawrence Seaway in 1959 stimulated the foreign trade of various lake ports, including Detroit.

Watch out for those windshields!

State Books & Websites

My First Book About Michigan by Carole Marsh
America the Beautiful: Michigan by Martin Hintz
From Sea to Shining Sea: Michigan by Dennis Fradin
Let's Discover the States: Michigan by the Aylesworths
Awesome Almanac: Michigan by Annette Newcomb
The Michigan Experience by Carole Marsh

MARVELOUS MICHIGAN WEBSITES

http://www.state.mi.us
http://info.migov.state.mi.us
http://mel.lib.mi.us
http://199.190.91.5/midir/main.htm
http://www.michiganexperience.com

Michigan
Glossary

abolitionist: person opposed to slavery

constitution: a document outlining the role of a government

dune: a rounded hill or ridge of sand that has been heaped up by the wind

fort: a building with strong walls for defending against an enemy

immigrant: a person who comes to a new country to live

pasty: pastry turnover with meat filling

peninsula: a piece of land surrounded on three sides by water

resources: a supply of something that takes care of a need

revolution: the overthrow of a government

seaway: an inland waterway to the sea for ocean ships

secede: to voluntarily give up being part of an organized group

Michigan
Spelling Bee

Here are some special Michigan-related words to learn! To take the Spelling Bee, have someone call out the words and you spell them aloud or write them on a piece of paper.

SPELLING WORDS

ancestors
Escanaba
Jesuit
Kalamazoo
Keweenaw
Mackinaw
Manistique
Marquette
Menominee
Michiganders
missionary
Ojibwa
Ontonagon

peninsula
Petoskey
Pontiac
Potawatomi
Republican
Sojourner Truth
sturgeon
Tahquamenon
territory
voyageurs
wolverine
Ypsilanti

Spelling List

About the Author

ABOUT THE AUTHOR...

CAROLE MARSH has been writing about Michigan for more than 20 years. She is the author of the popular Michigan State Stuff series for young readers and creator, along with her son, Michael Marsh, of "Michigan Facts and Factivities," a CD-ROM widely used in Michigan schools. The author of more than 100 Michigan books and other supplementary educational materials on the state, Marsh is currently working on a new collection of Michigan materials for young people. Marsh correlates her Michigan materials to Michigan's Social Studies Content Standards. Many of her books and other materials have been inspired by or requested by Michigan teachers and librarians.

The author dedicates this book to her husband, Bob Longmeyer, who has helped her with all the research ("and driving!") necessary to complete her more than 10,000 childrens' titles.